·THE CHRONICLES OF·
NARNIA
THE LION, THE WITCH AND THE WARDROBE

Narnia.com

The Lion, the Witch and the Wardrobe: The Quest for Aslan

ISBN: 0-00-720615-1

First published in the United States of America in 2005 by HarperKids Entertainment, a trademark of HarperCollins Publishers, 1350 Avenue of the Americas, New York, NY10019.

This edition published in Great Britain in 2005 by HarperCollins Children's Books, a division of HarperCollins Publishers, 77-85 Fulham Palace Road, Hammersmith, London W6 8JB.

Visit the HarperCollins Children's Books website at www.harpercollinschildrensbooks.co.uk

Book design by Rick Farley.

1 3 5 7 9 10 8 6 4 2

Printed in Italy.

THE CHRONICLES OF NARNIA

THE LION, THE WITCH AND THE WARDROBE

THE QUEST FOR ASLAN

Adapted by Jasmine Jones
Based on the screenplay by Ann Peacock and Andrew Adamson and
Christopher Markus & Stephen McFeely
Based on the book by C. S. Lewis
Directed by Andrew Adamson

HarperCollins *Children's Books*

CHAPTER ONE

Lucy Pevensie stared out the window glumly. The rain was falling so hard that she couldn't even see the green hills outside. Her brothers and sister and she had come to live in the countryside because of the air raids in London. England was at war, and the German army was dropping bombs on the city. London wasn't safe, so many families were sending their children to the country. Their mother had cried when Peter, Susan, Edmund and Lucy stepped up to the train that was to take them to live with Professor Kirke. He was an old man that the Pevensies didn't even know. But he had a big house with plenty of room for the four of them.

Professor Kirke also had a grouchy housekeeper

named Mrs Macready. She didn't like children. "No shouting," Mrs Macready said when the Pevensies walked into the house. "No running. No touching of the historical artifacts. And above all, there shall be no disturbing of the Professor."

At first Lucy didn't think she would mind the rules. After all, there was a huge yard and a forest to play in, a river to swim in, and all sorts of things to explore. But now she was stuck inside because of the rain. Her brothers and sister were bored, too.

"We could play hide-and-seek," Lucy suggested.

"Hide-and-seek's for kids," Edmund said. He was only three years older than she was, and he always tried to act more grown-up than he was.

"Come on, Peter," Lucy begged as she tugged on his shirt.

Peter sighed and looked down into Lucy's pleading face. He was the oldest and had promised Mum that he would look after the family. "One," he said slowly. "Two. Three."

Lucy and the others darted away.

The Professor's house was full of good hiding places. Lucy darted up the stairs and turned a corner

just in time to see her older sister, Susan, closing herself into a window seat.

"Thirty-one." Lucy could hear Peter's voice from downstairs.

Dashing towards the windows, Lucy ripped back a heavy velvet curtain. "I was here first," Edmund said, snapping the curtain back into place.

Hurrying down the hall, Lucy came to a closed door.

"Eighty-nine," Peter said.

Quickly, Lucy shoved the door open and went inside. The room was empty except for a large wardrobe that sat against the wall. She hurried over to it and yanked on the knob. Taking a deep breath, Lucy dived into the wardrobe. She was careful to leave the door open a little, though, because she knew that it could be dangerous to close herself in. She decided to hide deep among the coats, so she put out her hand to feel for the back of the wardrobe.

"Ouch!"

Lucy frowned. That was strange — she had touched something prickly.

She took a halting step forward. *Crunch.*

What was that? Lucy wondered. Feeling suddenly, strangely cold, she crunched forward through the darkness. In a moment Lucy came face-to-face with a pinecone hanging from a green tree branch.

Something cold but delicate brushed her cheek, and Lucy was surprised to realise that she was standing in a forest . . . and that it was snowing. There was a lamppost in the clearing in front of her.

Something crunched in the snow behind Lucy. Turning, she saw a very strange creature – he had legs like a goat and two horns growing out of a thick patch of curly hair on his head. He was wearing a red scarf and carried an umbrella in one hand and a bunch of packages wrapped in brown paper in the other.

The creature and Lucy let out a scream at the same time. The goat man hopped behind a tree.

"Are you . . . hiding from me?" Lucy asked after a moment.

The creature peeped out from behind the tree. "No . . . ," he said slowly. "I just didn't want to scare you."

"Oh. Thank you," Lucy said, although she knew the creature was more frightened than she was.

"You *are* odd looking," the goat man said. "For a Dwarf."

Lucy laughed. "I'm not a Dwarf," she told him. "I'm a girl!"

The creature gaped at her. "You mean to say you're . . . Human?"

"Of course," Lucy said.

The creature glanced around nervously.

"If you don't mind me asking," Lucy said, glancing at the creature's legs, "what are you?"

The creature sniffed, as though Lucy had asked a very silly question.

"I'm a Faun. Allow me to introduce myself. My name is Tumnus."

"Lucy Pevensie."

"Lucy Pevensie," Mr Tumnus said with a shy smile, "how would you like to come have tea with me?"

"Thank you very much," Lucy replied, "but I probably should get back."

Mr Tumnus held his umbrella over Lucy. "We'll have a roaring fire," he promised, "and toast, and hot tea, and cake."

Lucy giggled. "All right," she said at last. "I suppose

I could come for a while."

As Lucy and Mr Tumnus walked to his house, the Faun told her about Narnia, which was the name of the land she had wandered into. It had been winter in Narnia for a hundred years – always winter and never Christmas. Lucy thought that was very sad.

Mr Tumnus's house turned out to be made of rock and set next to some tall cliffs, almost like a cave. It was surprisingly warm and cosy inside.

The Faun offered Lucy toast and sardines, and the two of them sat down by the roaring fire as he began to play the flute. Suddenly Lucy began to feel very sleepy. She drowsed in her chair as figures played in the flames — a herd of Centaurs, a flying horse, and finally . . . a Lion.

The Faun stopped playing, and the fire went out.

"What time is it?" Lucy asked, her eyelids fluttering open. "I should be going."

Mr Tumnus was trembling. "I'm such a terrible Faun," he said softly. He twisted his flute in his hands as tears welled in his eyes. Lucy hopped off her chair and offered him her handkerchief.

"You can't have done anything that bad," Lucy said.

"It isn't something I have done, Lucy Pevensie. It's something I am doing."

Lucy felt frightened. "What are you doing?"

Mr Tumnus could barely whisper his answer. "I'm kidnapping you.

"The White Witch," Mr Tumnus went on. "It's because of her that it's always winter. She gave orders. . . ." He dabbed at his eyes with the delicate linen. "If we ever find a Human, we're supposed to turn it over to her."

Lucy's face trembled. "I thought you were my friend."

Suddenly, the Faun's face changed. He looked determined. "Come on," he said to Lucy. "We may not have much time."

Lucy and Mr Tumnus dashed through the woods to the lamppost. "No matter what happens, Lucy Pevensie," Mr Tumnus said, "I'm glad to have met you. You've made me feel warmer than I've felt in a hundred years."

Lucy smiled at her new friend and then hurried off into the forest. Finally, she felt dark fur coats against her face, and a moment later she tumbled out of the wardrobe.

"It's all right!" Lucy shouted as she burst through the door. "I'm back!"

CHAPTER TWO

Edmund poked his head out from behind the velvet curtain and sneered at Lucy. "Shut up," Edmund said. "He's coming."

A moment later Peter rounded the corner. He stared at them. "I'm not sure you two have got the idea of this game."

Susan popped out of her hiding place.

"Weren't you wondering where I was?" Lucy asked. She tried to explain that she had been gone for hours, but the other three looked confused. Her adventure had taken no time at all!

Lucy told the others about Narnia and her time

with Mr Tumnus, but they didn't believe her. So she dragged them to the wardrobe and opened it up.

Putting her hand between the coats, Susan knocked the back of the wardrobe. It was solid wood.

"We don't all have your imagination," Peter told Lucy.

"But I wasn't imagining!" Lucy insisted.

"I believe you," Edmund said. "Didn't I tell you about the cricket pitch in the bathroom cupboard?"

Lucy burst into tears and ran from the room.

Peter glared at his brother. "When are you going to grow up?"

"Shut up!" Edmund shouted. "You think you're Dad, but you're not!" He stormed out of the room.

Peter sighed. Taking care of the family was harder than he had thought it would be.

That night, Lucy had trouble sleeping. She knew the others thought that she was lying . . . but Narnia was real. But, if it was real, why wasn't it there when the others opened the wardrobe?

Lucy decided to have another look.

Quietly she crept out of bed and down the hall to

the wardrobe room. As she opened the door to the wardrobe, a cold gust of wind blew against her face. Narnia!

Lucy stepped inside.

But someone else was awake, too. Edmund saw Lucy go into the wardrobe room. He followed her inside, eager to tease his sister about her imaginary country.

Edmund yanked the wardrobe door open wide and shouted, "Boo!"

But he couldn't see Lucy.

"*Lu*-cy!" Edmund sing-songed as he stepped into the wardrobe. "I hope you're not afraid of the *da*-rk!" Pushing through the coats, he stepped forward . . . and saw a lamppost.

"Lucy?" Edmund whispered. His heart sank as he stared at the woods around him. Lucy had been right after all!

There was a soft jingling, and a moment later a sleigh pulled by white reindeer charged into the clearing. A mean-looking Dwarf leaped down from the sleigh and grabbed Edmund.

"What is it now, Ginarrbrik?" asked a woman's voice.

"Make him let me go!" Edmund cried.

"How dare you address the Queen of Narnia!" the Dwarf growled at Edmund.

Edmund's eyes went wide in fear. "I didn't know!"

"Stop!" shouted the Queen.

The Dwarf relaxed his hold, and Edmund stared up at the woman in the sleigh. Her face was white – white as the snow on the ground – and her eyes glittered green below an icy crown. She was the most beautiful woman Edmund had ever seen.

"What is your name, Son of Adam?" the Queen asked.

"Edmund."

She looked interested. "And how did you come to enter my dominion, Edmund?"

"I was following my sister – " Edmund began.

The Queen's eyebrows lifted. "There are more of you?"

"Four of us," Edmund said.

For a moment, Edmund thought that the Queen looked frightened.

"She met a Faun," Edmund went on, "called Tumnus."

"Edmund, dear," she said as she held out her hand. "Would you like something hot to drink?"

Edmund, who was very cold, said that he would.

The Queen took out a small copper bottle. She let a single drop of liquid fall onto the snow. A moment later, a steaming cup covered in jewels sat before Edmund. The Dwarf handed it to him, and Edmund took a sip. It was sweet and warm and foamy – and absolutely delicious.

"I can make anything you would like to eat," the Queen told him.

"Turkish Delight?" Edmund asked, and a moment later a box of the treats appeared before him. Edmund popped one into his mouth. Sweet and chewy, it was the best thing Edmund had ever tasted. He grabbed another piece.

"You know, Edmund," the Queen said, "I have no children. You're the sort of boy I could see one day becoming a Prince of Narnia. Or perhaps even King. Of course, you'd need to bring your family."

"I guess I could bring them," Edmund said, although he didn't like the idea that Peter might get to be King, too.

The Queen turned Edmund's head towards a pair of dark hills. "My house is right between them," she told him. "It has rooms simply filled with Turkish Delight."

Edmund looked down at the box. He had eaten all of the sweets. "Couldn't I have some more now?"

The Queen smiled. She knew that the Turkish Delight was enchanted — anyone who tasted it would want more and would do anything to get it. "We'll see each other again," she told Edmund, "won't we?"

"I hope so . . . Your Majesty," Edmund said.

Ginarrbrik cracked his whip, and the reindeer galloped away.

"Edmund?"

Turning, Edmund saw Lucy hurrying toward him. "Oh, Edmund, you got in, too."

Edmund wiped his mouth. He wasn't feeling very well after eating all of that Turkish Delight. "Where've you been?" he asked.

"With Mr Tumnus!" Lucy said. "He's fine. The White Witch hasn't found out anything about him meeting me. . . ."

Edmund realised she meant the Queen. He swallowed hard as he turned to follow Lucy out of the wardrobe.

"Peter and Susan will have to believe in Narnia now that we've both been here," Lucy said.

CHAPTER THREE

Lucy ran to tell Peter and Susan about Narnia. "It's all in the wardrobe like I told you," Lucy said with a smile. "Ask Edmund."

Everyone turned to Edmund. But suddenly Edmund felt that he didn't want to tell the others that he had talked to the White Witch. And he didn't want to admit that Lucy was right, either. "That's the problem with little kids," Edmund said. "They don't know when to stop pretending."

Lucy burst into tears and ran from the room. She could hear Peter and Susan running after her, but she didn't stop . . . until she ran into Professor Kirke.

Mrs Macready stepped into the hall. "You children are one shenanigan shy of sleeping in the stables!" she said as Peter and Susan appeared.

"It's all right," the Professor said kindly. He looked down at Lucy, who was still crying. "But I think this one is in need of a little hot chocolate."

Mrs Macready took Lucy's hand and led her towards the kitchen as the Professor gestured for Peter and

Susan to come into his office.

"We're very sorry, sir," Peter said.

"It's Lucy, sir," Susan explained. "She says she's found a magical land in the upstairs wardrobe."

The Professor's eyes sparkled. "What was it like?"

"Like talking to a lunatic," Susan said.

"Not her," the Professor said. "The place."

Peter and Susan stared at each other.

"You're not saying you believe her?" Peter asked. "Edmund said they were only pretending."

The Professor nodded. "And he's usually the more truthful one?"

Peter narrowed his eyes. "No . . ."

"So, you think Lucy's mad?" Professor Kirke asked.

Susan shook her head. "This has all been pretty hard on her, but I wouldn't go that far."

Professor Kirke filled his pipe. "Then, if Lucy isn't lying, and if she's not mad, then logically . . ." He eyed Susan. "We must assume she's telling the truth."

Peter and Susan gaped at him. "Impossible," Susan said.

"Now tell me," the Professor said as he pulled up a chair. "What did Lucy say . . . exactly?"

It was a beautiful day, but Edmund didn't feel happy. He stared up at Professor Kirke's house as Peter tossed him a cricket bat.

"Why can't we play hide-and-seek again?" Edmund asked. He was thinking of Narnia . . . and Turkish Delight.

"I thought you said it was a kid's game," Peter replied.

"We could all use the fresh air," Susan said as she looked over at Lucy, who sat beneath a tree, glumly brushing her doll's hair.

Grumbling, Edmund took his place at the wicket. When Peter bowled the ball, Edmund whacked it as hard as he could. It sailed through the air —

Crash! Clang!

The ball smashed through a leaded glass window in the library.

The Pevensies hurried inside to see the damage. The library carpet was covered in glass and a suit of armour lay across the floor, knocked over by the cricket ball.

Peter hurried to put the armour back together, but just then they heard footsteps in the hall.

"The Macready!" Susan whispered.

The Pevensies abandoned the armour and rushed out of the library through another door. They ran up the stairs, but Mrs Macready's footsteps were right behind them. They hurried down the hall — but her steps were before them. Finally, there was no choice. They ran into the wardrobe room.

"All right, then," Peter said, yanking open the door to the wardrobe. They scrambled inside. Peter put his

eye to the crack and saw the knob on the door turning. He hurried his sisters and brother deeper into the dark wardrobe.

"Peter," Susan asked after a minute, "are your trousers wet?"

Looking down, Peter realised that he was standing in a patch of snow. Susan stared up into the trees. "Impossible," she whispered.

"Don't worry," Lucy said. She was smiling for the first time in days. "I'm sure it's just your imagination."

Peter stared at Edmund. "You little liar."

"You didn't believe her, either," Edmund griped. Of course, Edmund realised that this was very different, as he had been to Narnia before and Peter hadn't.

"Apologise to Lucy," Peter said to his brother.

"All right," Edmund said. "I'm sorry." But he didn't mean it.

"Maybe we should go back," Susan said. She looked at Peter.

"I think Lucy should decide what we do," Peter said.

Lucy smiled. "I want you to meet Mr Tumnus."

It was very cold, so Peter took a few long fur coats

from the wardrobe rack. "If you think about it logically," Peter told Susan, "we're not even taking them out of the wardrobe."

Peter, Susan and Lucy laughed as they walked through the forest. Once Susan even fell. But instead of complaining, she just made an angel in the snow. Edmund was the only one who wasn't happy. He wanted Turkish Delight.

Lucy began to walk more quickly as they neared Mr Tumnus's house. "I'm sure he'll put on some tea, and he'll have cake and – " As she rounded the bend, Lucy stopped in her tracks. Mr Tumnus's door had been pulled off the hinges.

The Pevensies hurried inside. The walls were black with smoke, and the furniture had been smashed.

"Who would do something like this?" Lucy asked.

Leaning down, Peter picked up a piece of paper. "'The Faun Tumnus is hereby charged with High Treason against her Imperial Majesty Jadis, Queen of Narnia, for comforting her enemies and fraternizing with Humans,'" Peter read aloud. "'Signed Maugrim, Captain of the Secret Police.'"

"Now we really should go back," Susan said nervously.

"But what about Mr Tumnus?" Lucy asked. "This is all my fault. I'm the Human! She must have found out he helped me."

"If all he did was help you," Peter said, "then I'm sure this Queen will figure that out – "

"She's not a Queen," Lucy said angrily. "She's a Witch! We have to help him."

"Don't worry, Lucy," Peter said. "We will."

"And how do you propose we do that?" Susan demanded.

"Psst!"

The Pevensies looked at one another, then peered out the door. A very large Beaver crooked a finger at them. *"Psst!* Lucy?" the Beaver asked. He held out her handkerchief – the one Lucy had given to Mr Tumnus when she had visited before.

"Is he all right?" Lucy asked.

The Beaver looked around nervously. "That's better left for safer quarters." Suddenly he turned and hurried off. Lucy and the others followed him.

Mr Beaver led them through the forest until they came to a frozen river and a large dam. A large female Beaver opened a door that led inside the dam. When

she saw the Pevensies, she gasped and hurried over to them. "I never thought I'd live to see this day," she said, taking Susan's hand in her own. "Come inside, you must be starving."

Edmund cast a glance towards the dark hills in the distance. He could see a castle between them. Then he followed his sisters and brother into the dam.

Mrs Beaver bustled about, serving the Pevensies a delicious lunch of fried fish.

"There must be some way we can help Mr Tumnus," Peter said.

"Few who go through the Witch's gates ever come out." Mr Beaver shook his head.

Lucy's eyes filled with tears.

"There is hope, dear," Mrs Beaver told her gently.

"Oh, there's more than hope," Mr Beaver agreed. He leaned forward and whispered, "Aslan is on the move."

Even though none of the Pevensies knew who Aslan was, all of them felt instantly better the moment they heard his name. All of them, that is, except for Edmund, who felt horribly afraid.

"Who's Aslan?" Edmund asked.

"He's the real King of Narnia! And he's waiting for you at the Stone Table," Mr Beaver said. "There's a prophecy. They say that when two Sons of Adam and two Daughters of Eve arrive in Narnia, Aslan will return. Then, together, they will lead an army against the White Witch and restore peace to the land."

The children gaped at one another.

"And you think we're the ones?" Peter asked.

"You'd better be," Mr Beaver said.

"I think you've made a mistake," Peter told the Beavers. "We're not heroes."

"We really have to go," Susan added.

Lucy stared at them. "But what about Mr Tumnus?"

"Lucy," Peter said patiently, "it's time the four of us were getting home. Ed?" He looked at where his brother had been sitting . . . but Edmund was gone. "I'm going to kill him," Peter said crossly.

"You may not have to," Mr Beaver replied. "Has he ever been to Narnia before?"

Peter ran outside to find Edmund. Mr Beaver raced after him. "You've lost him to the Witch," the Beaver said. They could all see Edmund climbing the cliff toward the Witch's castle.

"Only Aslan can help your brother now," Mr Beaver said.

CHAPTER FOUR

The Beavers knew that the White Witch would send her secret police after them right away, so they packed a few provisions and hurried through a tunnel beneath the dam. They were headed for the Stone Table.

Once they reached a wood at the end of the tunnel, Mr Beaver grinned happily. "We're almost there," he said. "All we have to do is go over that frozen lake . . . then hike through those woods . . . then cross the Great River . . . climb some hills . . . until we reach that last hill there."

Peter, Susan and Lucy looked out at the hill. It seemed very small and far away.

They trudged forward through the snow.

The children felt like they had been marching forever when Mr Beaver turned and shouted. "Hurry up! Run! Run!"

Mrs Beaver jumped up and down. "It's *her!*"

Turning, the children saw a speeding sleigh bearing down on them, its bells ringing.

The Pevensies ran.

Mr Beaver led them to a small cave. "Inside!" he shouted. "Dive!"

The children and the Beavers hid in the small hole for a long time. Finally, Mr Beaver dared to go outside. The children held their breath, until they heard the sound of . . . laughter.

"Come up!" Mr Beaver called. "There's someone here to see you."

Peeking out of the hole, Lucy saw a tall man with a long white beard wearing a brilliant red robe. He wore a sword at his hip. Lucy grinned. "Merry Christmas, sir," she said.

Father Christmas smiled at her. "Merry Christmas, Lucy."

Susan stepped forward. "I thought there was no

Christmas in Narnia," she said.

"It has indeed been a long time," said Father Christmas. "But the hope you have brought us, your Majesties, is finally weakening the Witch's magic. Still . . . ," he said as he pulled a sack from his sleigh. "You could probably do with these."

"Presents!" Lucy cried.

Father Christmas gave Peter a sword and a shield. He gave Lucy a tiny dagger and a small vial. "One drop will cure any injury," he explained. And he gave Susan a bow, arrows and a horn. "This bow will never miss its mark," he explained. "And wherever you are when you blow this horn, help will come."

The children thanked Father Christmas as he climbed into his sleigh.

"Thank you, sir," Peter said.

"No. Thank *you*, my King," Father Christmas said. "Long live Aslan. And Merry Christmas." And then he rode away.

The Beavers led Peter, Susan and Lucy farther through the forest. With every step the air seemed to get warmer. Soon Lucy realised that the snow at her feet was turning to slush. Suddenly they came upon a cherry tree in full flower. Peter picked up a petal. "You know what this means?" he asked.

"Spring!" Lucy cried, excited.

But Peter did not look happy. "Yes," he said. "Spring."

They had planned to walk across the frozen surface of the Great River. But once they reached it, they saw that cracks had formed along the ice, and dark water swirled below.

"Our shortcut," Susan said, "is melting."

"We need to cross," Peter announced. "Now." Lucy and the Beavers followed him down the riverbank, but Susan hesitated. A moment later, a Wolf howl sliced through the air. Susan hurried after the others.

Soon, Peter saw two Wolves picking their way across the waterfall before him. One was Maugrim, the Captain of the Witch's Secret Police, and the other was Vardan, his second in command. They leaped directly in front of the Pevensies. Peter pushed Lucy behind him and drew his sword.

"Put that down, boy," Maugrim taunted. "Someone could get hurt. All my Queen wants is for you to take your family and go. Leave now, and your brother leaves with you."

"Maybe we should listen to him," Susan said.

"No, Peter!" Mr Beaver shouted as Vardan knocked him down. "Narnia needs you."

"What will it be, Son of Adam?" Maugrim asked.

Peter lowered his sword, about to give up — but at that moment, a huge chunk of ice fell from the top of the nearby waterfall, cracking the river's surface.

"Hold on to me!" Peter shouted. Susan grabbed his coat and reached for Lucy. With a quick stroke, Peter drove his sword into the surface of the ice.

A moment later, the waterfall burst. Peter held tight to the sword as the water crashed down on them. Susan and Lucy clung to Peter and rode the chunk of ice over

the water. The Beavers, who were very strong swimmers, managed to stay afloat — but the Wolves were washed away.

The Pevensies paddled to shore. On the other side of the river, Narnia was in full bloom. Yellow tulips burst from the green earth at Susan's feet.

For the first time in one hundred years, it was spring.

The air was sweet with the smell of flowers as Peter, Susan, Lucy and the Beavers made their way through the wooded hills. They hurried down to Aslan's camp, which was swarming with all sorts of creatures —

Centaurs and Talking Animals and Naiads and Dryads and Fauns like Mr Tumnus.

Peter walked up to a regal tent. "We have come to see Aslan," he told the Centaur Oreius, who stood guard.

Lucy gasped as an enormous, beautiful Lion stepped out of the tent. Everyone knew right away that this was Aslan himself – the rightful King of Narnia.

"Welcome, Peter, Son of Adam," Aslan said in his deep, rich voice. "Welcome, Susan and Lucy, Daughters of Eve. But where is the fourth?"

"That's why we're here, sir," Peter said to the Lion. "We need your help. Our brother has been captured. By the White Witch."

"He betrayed them," Mr Beaver told Aslan.

Aslan's gentle eyes landed on Peter's face. "Then why do you wish to help him?"

Peter swallowed hard. He felt guilty that Edmund had left. Peter was supposed to be keeping the family together. "It's partly my fault," he admitted. "I was too hard on him."

"We both were," Susan put in.

"And," Lucy added, "he's our brother."

"All shall be done for Edmund," Aslan promised.

"But it may be harder than you think."

Aslan and Peter walked away from the others, up the hill that overlooked the camp. As they looked east, Peter could just make out a castle glittering like a diamond in the distance.

"That is Cair Paravel," Aslan said, as though he had read Peter's mind, "the castle of the four thrones, in one of which you must sit, Peter. As High King."

Peter looked away. "Aslan . . ." he said. "I'm not who you think I am. I couldn't even protect my own family."

"You've brought them safely this far," the Lion replied.

"Not all of them." Peter's voice was quiet.

Aslan stopped. "Peter, I will do all that I can to help your brother." He gestured to the camp — to the hundreds of creatures that were preparing to fight the Witch. "But I, too, want my family safe."

Just then, a horn blasted through the air.

"Susan!" Peter cried. He ran down the hill and to the river, where Susan and Lucy were hanging from a tree, trying to escape from two ferocious Wolves — Maugrim and Vardan.

Peter drew his sword, and Maugrim snarled.

Aslan and Oreius arrived at that moment. Aslan

pinned Vardan to the ground as Peter and Maugrim circled each other.

"You may think you're a King," Maugrim growled. "But you're going to die like a dog!" He leaped, baring his fangs.

"Peter!" Lucy cried as her brother and the Wolf fell to the ground . . . and lay perfectly still.

Then Peter shoved Maugrim away. The Wolf was dead.

Aslan released Vardan, who leaped away into the forest. "Follow him," the Lion said to Oreius. "He'll lead you straight to his mistress."

Oreius and a squad of other Centaurs galloped after the Wolf.

When Susan and Lucy stumbled out of their tent the next morning, they saw that Peter was already awake – and staring out over the ridge. Lucy followed his gaze – and saw a boy walking alone with Aslan.

"Edmund!" Lucy cried. She started to run towards her brother, but Peter put a hand on her shoulder and stopped her. Soon Aslan returned with Edmund, who was hanging his head in shame.

The White Witch had treated Edmund very cruelly. She kept him prisoner and forced him to carry her loads as she made her way toward the Stone Table. Finally, she left him tied up near her camp in the woods, guarded by Ginarrbrik. Edmund was very grateful when Oreius and the herd of Centaurs found him and set him free.

"There is no need to speak to Edmund about what is past," Aslan said.

"Are you all right?" Susan asked. Edmund looked thin and pale — and filthy.

"I'm a little tired," Edmund admitted. Actually, he was more than a little tired — he was exhausted. He had hardly slept in days.

"Get some sleep," Peter told his brother. "And Edmund . . ."

Edmund looked at his brother hopefully.

"Try not to wander off," Peter said.

Like the rest of Aslan's army, the Pevensies started to get ready for war. Lucy practised with her dagger while Susan took aim with her bow. Nearby, two Centaurs showed Edmund and Peter how to charge an

enemy on horseback.

"Peter!" Mr Beaver called as he ran toward the brothers. "Edmund! The Witch has demanded a meeting with Aslan."

At that moment a horn blasted through the camp. Peter and Edmund looked over to see four one-eyed Cyclops carrying a platform that held the White Witch. A guard of Minotaurs marched behind her. Ginarrbrik ran ahead.

Susan and Lucy joined their brothers as they stood beside Aslan.

The Witch gazed at the Lion and smiled. "You have a traitor amongst you, Aslan," she said.

Edmund swallowed hard.

"His offence was not against you," Aslan replied in his quiet growl.

"Every traitor belongs to me," the Witch replied. "His blood is my property."

"What you say," Aslan told the Witch, "is true."

Edmund looked shaken, and Lucy was about to cry.

The Lion stared at the Witch. "I shall talk with you alone," he told her.

CHAPTER FIVE

"They're coming," Peter said. Aslan and the Witch had spent a long time in Aslan's tent. Now the Witch was grinning in triumph.

Aslan faced the crowd that had gathered before him. Then he turned to the children. "She has renounced her claim on your brother's blood."

Peter clapped Edmund on the shoulder as the Witch climbed onto her platform and was carried away.

"Will there still be a war?" Peter asked the Lion.

"Nothing has changed," Aslan told him. It was clear tomorrow would be a hard day.

* * *

That night, Susan and Lucy couldn't sleep. They stepped out of their tent and saw Aslan walking slowly into the woods with his head down, his tail dragging. With a terrible feeling in their hearts, Susan and Lucy followed him.

They hid in the bushes as the Lion trudged heavily to the Stone Table, where a crowd of horrible creatures waited for him. There were Ogres and Hags,

Minotaurs and Boggles – and at the end of the table . . . the White Witch.

The Witch grinned. "Behold," she said with a sneer, "the Great Lion."

Aslan did not protest as the creatures rushed at him, knocking him onto his back and tying his paws.

"Why doesn't he fight back?" Lucy whispered to her sister. She cried as the horrible creatures shaved Aslan's

beautiful golden fur. Then the Witch raised a dagger high.

The girls couldn't watch as the Witch drove her knife into Aslan's heart.

"The great Cat is dead!" the Witch shrieked. She turned to a cruel-looking Minotaur. "General, prepare your troops for battle."

Susan and Lucy held their breath as the Witch led her troops right past their hiding place. Once they were sure the evil crowd was gone, Susan and Lucy crept towards Aslan.

"He must have known what he was doing. . . ." Susan said as she looked at the Lion's lifeless face. Lucy wrapped her arms around Susan, and the sisters cried as though their hearts would never be mended.

Peter's heart sank as he listened to a Tree Spirit tell how Aslan had been murdered. Peter was filled with sadness — and fear. He knew that it was up to him to lead Aslan's army against the Witch, but he didn't think that he could do it.

"That army is ready to follow you," Edmund told his brother. "And so am I."

Peter took a deep breath. Then he stepped outside where Oreius and Mr Beaver stood waiting with a handful of soldiers. "Gather your troops and strike camp," Peter told them. "We march within the hour."

"And Aslan?" Oreius asked.

"We must do what he has asked of us," Peter replied. "We will meet the Witch in battle. Without Aslan."

CHAPTER SIX

Susan and Lucy sat with Aslan for a long time. Slowly the sky grew pale above them.

"He looks better in the light, doesn't he?" Lucy asked.

Susan looked down at the camp, where Aslan's army was getting ready for battle. "We should go," she said.

The two sisters began to walk away from the Stone Table. But just as they turned their backs, there was a low rumble behind them, then a sound like an explosion. The ground shook with the blast. The Stone Table had cracked in half . . . and Aslan had disappeared.

"Is this more magic?" Susan asked.

"Perhaps it is," said a huge, warm voice behind the girls.

Turning, Susan and Lucy saw Aslan – bigger and even more golden than before. They flung their arms around him, burying their faces in his fur.

"But we saw the knife," Susan protested. "The Witch – "

"The Witch knows of the Deep Magic," Aslan said. "But there is a magic older than time itself. It is based not upon laws, but upon what is right and what is wrong. When a willing victim who has committed no treachery is killed in a traitor's stead, the table will crack and even death itself will turn backwards." He smiled at the girls. "Climb on my back and hold tight," Aslan said. "We have far to go, and little time to get there." With a huge leap, Aslan began to race across the countryside.

A trumpet sounded, and the Witch's army approached. She stood at the back of a gleaming chariot pulled by two white polar bears. Lifting his sword, Peter turned and pointed it at the Witch across the field. Hooves thundered as her army charged.

"For Narnia! For Aslan!" Peter shouted as his Unicorn and he plunged into the fight. They were surrounded by arrows, swords, talons and claws – every creature was fighting in its own way. From her chariot, the Witch used her wand to turn Aslan's creatures to stone.

Peter's Unicorn galloped ahead, fighting off Werewolves. With a fierce blow Peter knocked the Witch from her chariot. A moment later Peter fell from his saddle and found himself surrounded by Ogres.

While his back was turned, the Witch closed in on Peter, her wand held high.

In a flash, Edmund charged her, bringing his sword down on her wand. It snapped in two. The Witch stabbed Edmund with the jagged edge.

Suddenly an enormous Lion appeared at the top of a nearby cliff. It was Aslan. He had taken Susan and Lucy to the Witch's palace, where they had found hundreds of good creatures – including Lucy's old friend, Mr Tumnus – whom the Witch had turned to stone. A single breath from Aslan had made the creatures come alive – and now they were descending onto the battlefield with the Lion in the lead.

With one glance at the Lion and his troops, the White Witch's army turned and fled. Aslan pounced on the Witch, driving her into the ground.

"Peter!" Susan cried as she and Lucy joined him on the suddenly quiet battlefield.

"Where's Edmund?" Lucy asked.

"Edmund!" Susan shouted. A moment later, she spotted him — lying on the ground, with the Witch's wand buried between his ribs. Peter, Susan and Lucy raced to their brother's side.

Lucy pulled out her tiny vial, the gift from Father Christmas, and fell to her knees beside Edmund. She let a tiny drop fall onto his lips. A moment later Edmund

smiled weakly at her. He was alive.

Then Lucy went to the other wounded creatures and gave them each a drop from her vial. Aslan breathed on the ones the Witch had turned to stone.

The war was over. The prophecy had been fulfilled.

Many years later, long after Aslan had crowned Peter, Susan, Edmund and Lucy as Kings and Queens of Narnia, Peter hurried onto the balcony at Cair Paravel. He was much older now, and his hair and beard were wild. "The White Stag has been seen in Narnia," he said to his sisters and brother.

The White Stag granted wishes, so Susan, Edmund and Lucy rushed to their horses and galloped after Peter. They rode past the Stone Table and into the forest. Deep, deep into the woods they rode, over hills, through clearings, until finally they came to . . . a lamppost.

"What is this?" Edmund asked.

"'Tis a tree," Susan said, "of iron."

Peter dismounted and stared at the lamppost. "By the Lion's mane," he said, "it works upon me strangely."

"As if in a dream," Lucy agreed.

All four Pevensies climbed off of their horses. Just then the White Stag burst from the brush, and the Kings and Queens of Narnia dashed after it. The wood grew darker and quieter. The Pevensies had to hold out their hands to feel where they were going.

"These are not branches," Peter said after a while.

"They're . . . coats," Lucy said.

And in the next moment the Kings and Queens tumbled out of the wardrobe and back into the Professor's house — young again, and in their old clothes.

The doorknob turned, and Professor Kirke walked into the room. He stared at the children, who were piled in a heap on the floor. "What were you all doing in the wardrobe?" he asked.

"You would not believe us if we told you, sir," Peter said.

Professor Kirke smiled and tossed Peter a cricket ball. "Try me," he said.